THE UNTOLD WARS

by Maleko Kamahalohanuilai

DORRANCE
PUBLISHING CO
EST. 1920
PITTSBURGH, PENNSYLVANIA 15238

The contents of this work, including, but not limited to, the accuracy of events, people, and places depicted; opinions expressed; permission to use previously published materials included; and any advice given or actions advocated are solely the responsibility of the author, who assumes all liability for said work and indemnifies the publisher against any claims stemming from publication of the work.

Dorrance Publishing Co
585 Alpha Drive
Pittsburgh, PA 15238
Visit our website at *www.dorrancebookstore.com*

ISBN: 978-1-6366-1604-9
eISBN: 979-8-88604-918-3

PART 1

CHAPTER 1

The Tribe Men, Magi, and Zion

"Hikuuuuu! Where is that brat?" shouts Gen with a loud, deep voice.

Then a voice from the shadow replies to Gen, "Who you calling a brat, you old, bearded, washed-up warrior?"

Gen turns around and sees Hiku standing in the shadow under a tree leaning on its trunk looking at Gen, Gen then shouts in a loud tone full of rage, "OLD, BEARDED, WASHED-UP WARRIOR? WHY YOU LITTLE PIECE OF MANURE, I'M GONNA SMASH THAT PRETTY FACE IN…RHAAAAA!"

Gen takes off forward towards Hiku.

"Enough!" a voice says to Gen, and when Gen hears this voice, he immediately stops and turns around and responds Chief, then walks away, muttering angry words under his breath. "And Hiku, you shouldn't be provoking Gen. He is and still is the mightiest warrior in our tribe. Let's take a walk, son."

"So what, Pops, are you going to scold me about what I said to Gen earlier?"

"No, Hiku. I wanted to tell you how proud I am about how far you have come with your training, and I'm looking forward to you mastering the last two weapons of our tribe, then you will have the final duel to place you in the ranks of a True Born warrior."

Hiku then asks, "Father, why do we have to master five different weapons? All the other tribes only master one."

"Well, son, since the beginning of all the tribes, our tribe is the only tribe that practices this style, and not only that; we trained and taught the other tribe how to use and forge their weapons. Why do you think we are the strongest out of all seven tribes?" He looks at Hiku and sees that he is still puzzled and doesn't understand. Chief Ronn says, "Son, let me put it this way: would you rather have one tool that can do only one thing, or many to do a lot more?"

Hiku sits and thinks about it before answering, then he replies, "Well, what if there was one tool that could do more than just that one thing? Then you would have one that can do it all."

Chief Ronn shakes his head then looks around and sees Keno. Chief Ronn yells out, "Hiku and Keno, the two top students! How about an educational sparring match to show your Chief first-hand a look at your improvement?"

Hiku and Keno stare at each other from afar, then within an instant, Hiku throws two throwing axes towards Keno then dashes forward with great speed.

At a low stance with his sword drawn, Keno dodges one throwing axe and blocks the other with his twin dagger, then in a split second, both of them clash with one another. Hiku swings his sword upward; Keno blocks it with a downward cross block and back flips then launches both daggers at Hiku. Hiku blocks the dagger and continues to rush Keno. As soon as Keno touches the ground, he has his spear drawn and at the ready, then he dashes forward with his spear, thrusting it towards Hiku multiple times, the both of them firing at each other. Keno then does a triple thrust; Hiku dodges and blocks the attack then fires back with a series of strikes at Keno, but Keno manages to block the ongoing sword barrage from Hiku, and the clash between the two continues.

Moments later, Keno does an 360-degree jump back-spin and throws his spear at Hiku. Keno's spear has such a heavy impact with all that momentum, it disarms Hiku of his sword. Hiku quickly draws his spear and knocks away the two throwing axes that Keno had thrown after launching his spear. Keno draws his sword, and Hiku grips his spear, both staring at each other, getting ready for the next encounter, then a second later, both of them dash forward again, but before they make contact, Hiku does an aerial assault, flipping over Keno and striking in mid-air. When Hiku lands, he throws his spear at Keno and rushes forward behind his spear with his double daggers.

Keno blocks the aerial attack, spins around the thrown spear and then—

Chief Ronn yells, "Enough!" and both of them stop with in less than a half-inch away from a fatal blow towards each other. Chief Ronn starts to laugh, "Hahahaha," then says, "Keno, Hiku, great match. You two had my own blood boiling with all this intense fire you both have. WHOOO."

Gen runs in out of breath and says, "Chief, the beacon on the Secret Hill has been lit."

"Are you sure, Gen?"

Gen replies, "Yes, and not only that; the other tribes have called a meeting about this matter."

"Well then let us get ready to head to the Halls of Our Father and see what is in store for us, Gen. Let's go."

"Yes, Chief."

THE MAGI

Eastern High Mountain

At 7:45, the bells ring, and all the students head to their class.

"GOOOOOOOD MORNING, CLASS," Ms. Shenail yells out with energy and cheerfulness, then continues with the same tone, "It's 8 AM, and who's ready to have a lot of fun? 'Cause what better way is there to start off our morning then with a pop quiz! Okay, ready, class? Lola, come on down to the white board. You are our first pick for the day."

Lola walks over to the board and waits for Miss Shenail question for her.

"All right, Lola, you will have to draw out the symbol of the element. Here we go... What is fire?"

Lola turns and draws: ~/

"Great, now water."

~~

"Earth..."

^^

"Wind..."

{{

"Good job, Lola! Now, Ryan what's the verbal term for water?"

Ryan calls out, "Wai."

"Yes; now, Gordon, what about fire?"

"It's Ahi, Ms. Shenail," Gordon answers and then continues on with a bored tone of voice, "and Earth is Aina, wind is Makani. Now can we move on to the next lesson that we don't know of yet?"

"Well look at Mr. Smarty pants here getting ahead of himself," Ms. Shenails answers in a cheerful and goofy way, then she says, "Gordon, the pop quiz ain't over yet, silly!" Then she turns her head to Ry and asks, "Can you tell me how many magic classes there are, and what they are capable of?"

"We have four different type of magic user. First is the Enchanter, and they have the ability to enchant any type of object and turn them into one of four elements for attacking and projecting magic. Second is the Wizard. They have two different classes: one uses a wand to draw out a symbol and uses its right verbal term at the same time to create magic that is directed by their wand; the other wizard class uses verbal spell while holding there spell book. Third, we have the mage. They use a staff for close combat and can use verbal magic, and the rest is still unknown to us young adults. And the last of them are known as the Grand Ones, and I only know they are the strongest of all of them..."

A voice speaks out from the far corner of the classroom in a grim voice, "The Grand One is the only Magi that can use all magic, and only three out of 100,000 are born, and their bloodline is the creator of the Magi bloodline."

"Well, well, well, I very much appreciate you stepping in and sharing, Gedeon," Ms. Shenail tells him. "Okay that is enough for the pop quiz in the morning, but after lunch. you bet there will be more coming your way."

A loud noise comes from outside the classroom, and the students all get up to see what was going on.

"Now, now, class get back to your seats. I'm sure there is nothing to see…" As Ms. Shenail looks out the window, she sees two seniors standing across from each other getting ready to fight. One is a Mage, and the other is a Wizard.

The Mage yells out, "You Wizards are weaker than us! That's why you are the ones under us, and we under the Grand Magi."

Once the Wizard heard what the Mage had to say, he then yells out, "Wai spear!" and launches his attack towards the Mage. The Mage plants his feet and slams the bottom of his staff on the ground and yells out, "Aina wall!" then a huge wall shoots up from the ground, blocking the Wizard's attack.

Then the Mage lifts up his staff spin it over his head and grabs it then thrusts it forward while yelling, "Ahi Vi!" and a flock of 10 fire birds fly towards the Wizard in two rows.

The Wizard begins reading a spell out of the spell book that he carries with him, but before he can finish his spell, Ms. Shenail takes the book and another person out of nowhere dispels the Mage's attack.

"Both of you to my office, and thank you, Ms. Shenail, for stopping that spell. Who knows what could have happened."

"I should be thanking you. That flock of birds was pretty close, so thanks, Principal Hector."

"Shenail, can I have a word with you?"

Without looking at the person, Shenail replies, "Yes, Grand One."

"Shenail, are you familiar with the Secret Hill of the Tribesman?"

Shenail replies, "Yes, it is the hilltop that they use to signal the other tribes if there is great trouble."

"You are right, Shenail, but it puzzles me… Why is it lit now?"

ZION

Western Sky

"All teams, target in site. Charley team, take the right; Delta, cover the left; Bravo, you got the center, and Alpha, we do this as a team. It ain't a one-team show. All teams copy?"

Charley, Delta, and Bravo respond, "Roger that, Leader."

"Alpha, do you copy?"

No response.

Meanwhile, with the Alpha Team Leader and Alpha Team…

"Alright, Alphas, let's bag it up quick and head home. WHO'S THE ALPHAS?" shouts out the leader.

"WE THE ALPHAS," responded to the team.

"Alpha 2 and 3, come from the right, and 4 and 5, take the left. I'll hit the center. Get it done, Alphas.

Back with the other teams…

The Bravo Team Leader says, "Those damn Alphas… Do they know they're the only eyes we have in the sky? Those pricks."

The Charlie Team Leader replies, "Yeah not to mention if they get killed or trapped, we wouldn't know if where surrounded or if the enemy is expecting us—those jerks."

The Delta Team Leader interjects, "Guys, keep off the comm, and keep silent, or you both will give our location away, then we'll be really screwed. Keep your eyes peeled, and keep moving towards the last known location of the target."

"Roger that," Bravo and Charlie team leaders reply. "Roger that."

With the Alpha Team…

"Alpha 3, enemy located; begging my approach."

"Roger that, Alpha 3. Alpha 4 on the assist."

"Alpha Leader, this is Alpha 2. I got no visual on target; anybody got eyes on target?"

"Alpha 5 reporting negative, Alpha 2; no sign of them."

"Alpha Team, pull up! It's a trap! This is Alpha 3; my wing's been clipped. I'm going down! There are more than five of them—there's more like a hundred of them!

"Alpha 4 heading to your location, Alpha 3."

Alpha 4 lands next to Alpha 3.

"We are surrounded. Are you ready, 3?"

"Ha, I'm ready. Your number comes after me, so I should be asking you that question, 4."

"Enough with that crap. Any second, we will be engaged upon." Then from the shadows of the trees, arrows began flying out from everywhere. Alpha 4 yells out to Alpha 3, "Get down!" As soon as Alpha 3 ducks, Alpha 4 does a 360-degree spin using his metal wings that are strapped to his back to block and then shield both of the Alphas. Alpha 4 then radios out, "This is Alpha 4, Alpha 3's wings are damaged, and he can't fly out. I'll give him a lift, but if I make a move, I will be done for. I'm in need of a clearing, so I can get airborne with Alpha…"

"Hang on Alphas 3 and 4, I should be there in 3—2—1." Then a loud crackling noise struck near both the Alphas, followed by the sound of metal clashing. "Now Alpha 4, you're clear."

"Thanks, Alpha Leader…"

"Simulator shutting down…"

"WHAT WAS THAT? ALPHA TEAM, I TOLD YOU NOT TO LONE WOLF IT, AND YOU LONE WOLF IT! THEN YOU GET ONE OF THE WINGS DAMAGED, AND NOT ONLY THAT,

YOU GOT THE REST OF THE TEAMS KILLED. WHAT THE F—!"

The Alpha Leader speaks up, "Well, Mission Control, to be fair, you planted more troops in the testing right before Alpha 3 was about to take out the target, then you created more blind spots than anything, so me and my team couldn't get an accurate look at our surroundings, SIR."

"Well, you Alphas, so-called the best, but look how the best have fallen then spit, and just so you know, Alpha Leader, no one added anything during the testing. Because you left Bravo, Charlie, and Delta behind, they never saw the scouts that were ahead of them that alerted THE REST OF THEIR ARMY THAT SET A TRAP FOR YOUR DUMBASS."

"Commander, you are needed at the control center ASAP for briefing."

"All teams dismissed."

CHAPTER 2

The Lit Beacon

In the meeting at the Halls of Our Fathers...

Chief Ronn walks in and heads straight to the other tribes. Standing tall with Gen by his side, he says, "So why is a beacon that hasn't been lit for a hundred years on fire right now? Who lit the beacon of war and summoned this meeting? Which one of you did this?"

"We thought it was you, Chief Ronn, we all got here, and you weren't here yet, so we thought you were still returning from the Secret Hill."

"No, I just got news of this yesterday. How long have you all known?" Chief Ronn yells out.

"We saw the beacon lit one day ago," Chief Razor of the Eastern tribe replies.

The Chiefess Ale of the southern tribe says, "That is the same time we noticed it as well."

And then another chief says, "Yeah, I know for sure it was lit one day ago 'cause I was sitting with my son telling him the stories of old, and I was pointing right at the Sacred Hill when the beacon lit and headed straight here from the west."

Chief Razor then says, "Where is the Smith Tribe? Why are they not here?"

Chief Ronn shouts out, "The Smith Tribe has never been a part of any warfare, so if any tribe got a problem with them, let me settle this feud here and now. Any takers!"

A voice came from above the meeting and spoke in a grim tone, "So that would fix the problem at hand."

All the chiefs looked towards the voice and saw an elderly man standing on a ledge looking down at them. Quickly, all the Chiefs pound their right fist over there heart and say, "Father."

"Always trying to see who is stronger than the other instead of solving the real problem, but let me tell you this: the problem ain't with any of your Kin."

After the Father gave them his advice, he turned around and headed back into the dark part of the hall. Chief Ronn stepped forward and volunteered to go and inspect the beacon with Gen.

"I will be going as well," Chief Razor announces, then he tells his right-hand man to head back and ready the tribe for war. Then he tells Chief Ronn,"Don't you want your tribe to be ready, Ronn?"

"My tribe is born ready, Razor. Let's get going, Gen. And try to keep up, Razor."

Meanwhile, in Principal Hector's Office…

"Close my door and walk forward." The door gently closes behind them as they walk closer to the voice that is in the room. "Now tell me, did you light the beacon before you made that scene?"

The two seniors say, "Yes, Principal Hector."

"Good, good, hehehehehe!"

"So when do we meet our new teacher, Principal Hector?"

"Soon, child, soon, hahahahaha! Return to class, you two, and I'll be in touch with the both of you." The two seniors walk out of the office, and as soon as the door closes, a person walks out from the shadow and whispers in Hector's ears, "You know what to do next, Hector."

He replies, "Yes," then heads to the Secret Hill to makes sure that things go according to plan,

In the central part of Zion City…

"Alpha Team, we got an assignment, so listen up. A beacon has been lit in a lower terrain below. Back then, in the Great War, the Tribesmen would light this beacon to call all the other tribes and prepare for war, but we are not at war at this time, so this mission is an intel, and intel only, mission. Avoid all contact, and do not engage. I repeat: Do not engage. We want to know if they are preparing for war, and if so, with who. Got it?"

The Alpha Team replies, "Yes, Sir!"

The commander walks forward and calls for Alphas 2, 3, 4, and 5.

"Good luck on your mission, Alpha Leader. You need to fix the wings you lost in your last mission."

Alpha Leader runs up to the Commander, and before he can say anything, the Commander turns and tells him, "Have a good day, son," and closes the door.

Alpha leader yells out in anger and hits the wall a few times, then starts walking away.

After the briefing, Alpha Team gears up and waits for the green light to go.

"This is Mission Control. Are you mission ready?"

Alpha 2 radios back, "Wings are on and ready to fly, Mission Control."

"Wait, we have a problem: one of the wings is missing."

"WHAT? THAT DAMN ALPHA LEADER. This is Mission Control, Alpha 2, you find your team leader, and 3, you and 4 both go to that Hill and get whatever intel you can, 5, thank your team leader for this. Get those damaged wings to the repair shop."

On top of the Secret Hill…

"Gen, be ready, and Razor, don't lose your head. I sense the presence of our enemy," says Chief Ronn. Then all the sudden, fireballs and arrows come from different directions. Gen and Razor both deflect the attack with their masterful skills, and then Chief Ronn does a double slash windshear towards their enemy to cut open a path then tells Gen and Razor, Go!"

Both of them run towards the direction that was cleared, then Chief Ronn uses a shoulder blast to push the two over and down the hill, then yells, "Warn the tribe about the Magi ambushes!"

Then the Chief turns around and looks at the enemy, then roars and charges forward, swinging and smashing through his enemies.

Alpha Leader flies over the right side of the Secret Hill and hears a loud roar, then heads in that direction to see what's going on; but before he can get to where he heard the sound, spears and axes fly at him. He dodges the attack but then is brought down by a magical blast from the shadow. Alpha Leader hits the ground and rolls up back to his feet, gripping his spear and looking around him.

From the bushes comes out a large group of Tribesmen walking towards him, and all the sudden, Alpha 2 lands next to him.

"Get out of here now, before you get trapped! Leave now and report to headquarters."

"But what about you?" Alpha 2 says.

Alpha leader tells him, "There is no time. They are too close! Leave now! That's an order!"

Alpha 2 takes off with a smile and then radios command, "Alpha Leader is down and surrounded by the enemy. Permission for Alpha Team to engage the enemy?"

"Negative, Alpha Team. Report back, and do not engage. Alpha Leader put himself there; he can get himself out of it. Return home, Alpha Team, roger that?"

"Roger that."

Alpha Leader stares down his enemy, and from the corner of his eye, he sees a wavelike spell is cast, swallowing everything in its path. Then a voice calls out, "Hurry, this way; follow me!"

Alpha Leader runs towards the unknown voice and follows him into a mangrove that is very thick and swampy. They continue farther in, then come to a stop. Alpha Leader approaches the stranger, asking him who he is, why is he here, and why are the tribes all at the Hill.

"Do they want war?"

The stranger looks up and responds, "I'm no one you need to know about. I came here to investigate, and I have no clue why the Tribesmen were there, but I can tell you that only three Tribesmen were there. Whatever else was there is why I'm here."

"But from what I can tell, I saw maybe three tribes; not three men. Are you blind?" Alpha Leader says in confusion.

"No, you are the one who's blind," says the unknown man standing in front of him. "There is something else at play, and I hope it ain't what I think it is, but you must go back to your leader and give him this."

"How am I supposed to get back? My wings are damaged."

"I can teleport you there, but remember to give this to your leader."

"Why should I trust you? I don't even know you."

"Listen here, you Zion hothead, the three tribes you saw were wiped out a hundred years ago during the Great War between all, so take these back to your leader, and he will understand—Rii sii kii gii tii…" Alpha Leader disappears. "Now to the Chief," the unknown mage says to himself and takes off.

"Come on, you girly Magi, is that all you got?" Chief Ronn says aloud while laughing and standing over a pile of dead magies. Then all the sudden, a solar beam comes from the Hunted Grove and opens a path to Chief Ronn, and the unknown Magi yells, "Hurry! This way."

Chief Ronn respond, "I'll hurry, alright, to smash your skull in and split it in two, you damn magi!" Then Chief Ronn dashes forward and swings his sword with great power. It is so powerful that when the magi blocks, it the tree around them is cut down in an instant.

The unknown magi says, "I won't be able to block another hit like that, and I won't attack 'cause you are not my enemy."

Chief Ronn lowers his sword and then asks, "So who is your enemy?"

The unknown mage asks Chief Ronn, "Does this look familiar to you?" and shows him the banner.

Chief Ronn exhales and says, "Why do you have the banner of three fallen tribes from a hundred years ago?"

The unknown magi says, "Come with me, and we will find out this answer together."

CHAPTER 3

The Necromancer

The Necromancer speaks in low but high, grim voice, and says, "How did you fair, Hector?"

Hector replies, "Everything went according to plan, my Lord."

"When I ask how things went, I want to know in detail how it went, so again, how did YOU FAIR, HECTOR!"

"I can't breathe, my Lord..." The Necromancer opens his fist, and Hector gasps for air and catches his breath. "We lit the beacon on the Secret Hill, which caught the attention of the three factions; the Tribesmen, the Mages, and the Zion. Once they noticed this, they sent in a small group of warriors. The Tribesmen sent three warriors, two chiefs and a general. They were attacked by our Mage army, but one of the Chiefs created an open path with just a swing of his blade and then pushed the other two who were with him over the side of the cliff, and he stood behind. The Zion sent four flyers, and I shot down one, and he was surrounded by our tribe's army. While he was on the ground, one of his men landed by him then took off. Right now as we speak, they all are preparing for war against each other."

"Good boy, Hector, now that is a report. Now, take your leave and move to the next step of our plan."

A holographic call appears to Molath.

"How is your journey coming along? We await progress."

Molath the Necromancer replies to his King, "Everything is going according to plan. I have run into a fishing village and farms alongside the coast, and they will be more than happy to be a part of your kingdom; and now I'll be heading out to go beyond the open sea, my King."

"Great job, Molath. You bring even more resources to my kingdom. Have a safe journey."

Molath walks into a room that has three mirrors and looks to the mirror on the left, and his reflection says to Molath, "We will be bringing more than just resources back to the kingdom; but our very own army!"

And then Molath laughs and laughs and laughs.

CHAPTER 4

The Calm Before the Storm

"GRAB HIM! TAKE HIM DOWN! Welcome back, Alpha Leader, we've been waiting for you, throw him in the dungeon."

Down in the dungeon...

"Psst, wake up! Come on wake up, get up, Alpha Leader..."

"Oh man, where am I...?" As Alpha Leader tries to regain his senses, his eyes finally open and sees Alpha 3 and 5 in the same dungeon. "Why are you two locked up?" he asks.

"I stood against what Alpha 2 was saying about what happened on our last mission to the Secret Hill."

"And 5?"

"All I said was, 'Let's wait for Alpha Leader,' then *bam!* in the dungeon, I go. What did you do?"

"It's not about what I did, but what I can stop; 3 and 5, we need to break out and get these three banners that were given to me by a Mage to our leader, and he will understand."

"King Treon, preparation is complete."

"Great job, Alpha 2, and from this day forward, you will be Alpha Leader, and here is the new Alpha crew. Get to know them, Alpha Leader."

“Alpha Team, form up. I am Alpha Leader. You will only call me Alpha Leader and nothing else, and I will only call you by your Alpha number, and you will do the same. Is that clear?”

The Alphas respond, “YES, ALPHA LEADER.”

Back in the hunted grove…

“So, Magi, how long do we have to keep walking in this muck? I have to get back to my village and ready my people for war.”

“No, Chief Ronn, you need to go to the mountains of the Magies and let them know of this foul play, and if you don’t, another war is going to break out, and this war will be greater than the last, so please, will you go?”

“I am a Chief, not a messenger, Magi, and why don’t you go and let them know yourself? I have a duty, and that is to protect my people, so this is where we part ways.”

“Listen, Chief Ronn, you say your duty is to your people and to protect your people, then believe me when I say this, you are doing more than protecting your people; you are saving this world, and this can only be done by the mightiest warrior, so will you protect more than just your own people? Will you save them and everyone else, or slowly watch your bloodline be killed one after another till the last? What is your decision, Ronn?”

“It’s Chief Ronn to you, and why can’t you go?”

The Magi replies, “Well, like I said, this matter needs the mightiest warrior and another needs the wisest of all the Magis, so go there, show them this, and say you were sent by Mana. I will teleport you near the Magi Circle, rii sii kii tii—” and Chief Ronn disappears. “Good luck, heroes, may we meet at the end.”

War Ready

“Chiefs and chiefess, ready your warriors, for what has taken place on our Secret Hill was an act of war by the Magis. Chief Ronn stayed back, so I and Gen could warn the tribes of this, but Gen couldn’t leave his Chief behind, so he went back for him. As of right now, I have sent a messenger to the True Born tribe to inform them about what has happened and to tell the Chief's son, Hiku, to ready his warriors for the war that is at hand. I, too, will be leaving the hall of our father to ready my warriors."

"Chief Razor, what did you see when you were there on the hill top?"

"An army of Magis, fireballs and arrows came from all directions, me and Gen cancelled out the oncoming attack, and then Chief Ronn swung his sword, cutting everything down in one direction, then Chief Ronn yelled, 'This way quick,' then next thing you know, we were falling off the side of the cliff, and the rest I have already told you."

Chiefess Leila says, "But that doesn't make sense since… Fireballs, yes, but arrows? That's new."

"We don't have time for this. All tribes, Chiefs, and Chiefess will meet at the eastern borders on the fifth moon and prepare our attack on the Magis."

Back on Zion in the Dungeon...

"Well, 3 and 5, any idea on how we get out?"

"Well, me and 5 tried everything. The only thing we didn't try was asking them to open the door."

5 starts yelling, "Hey, guard, can you come here? I have something to ask you. Guard, guard!" Then a loud crashing noise comes from the stairway, and the guard falls to the ground knocked out. A voice that is very familiar to all of them spoke from afar.

"Hey, 5 and 3, I see you found 1, huh?"

5 and 3 yell, "It's 4, now hurry up and get us out before shit hits the fan."

"Shit already has hit the fan," 4 says while opening the cell, and as 1 passed 4, he tells him, "It's Alpha Leader, remember that 4?"

"So what has been going on since we been locked up?" Alpha Leader asked 4.

4 replies, "Well, the whole Zion is getting ready for war. They sent out three teams to the ground to establish a base. The new Alpha Team is leading the mission. They have already cleared out about 100 acres, and after they clear another 100 acres, the first battalion will be heading down and setting up base. It seems like we may be making an on-ground city, and apart from that, the Lord has signed a decree that allows Alpha Leader to make any decision and perpetration as he sees fit, so all of this, the Lord has no clue what's going on, so yeah. Alpha Leader, that is what been going on since the last day I saw you."

"Well I was down on the Secret Hills, and I was surrounded by Tribesmen, and I swear I was going to die, but then all the sudden, a Magi cut a path open towards the hunted grove, and I ran towards the Magi, then we headed deeper into the grove. When we came to a stop, we talked about what happened on the hilltop and then he said to me that all the Tribesmen that I saw belonged to tribes that were wiped out during the Great War between all; then he gave me these and said show them to our leader, then zapped me right in front of those guards."

"Wait, so what did he mean by they were from tribes that were wiped out?" Alpha 5 asks.

"Well, the only way to find out is to get to our Lord, so enough talking. Time to get moving, Alpha Team."

"YES, ALPHA LEADER."

Preparation

"Hey Principal Hector, how is your day going?"

"Well, it just got even more interesting, Ms. Sheila. Gather the teachers, and let's meet in the Great Hall. We must hurry, Ms. Sheila."

"I'll get right on it, Principal." *My he is so hyper what could be happening?* she wondered.

Within the Great Hall behind a secret door…

"So, Tribesman, tell me who was it that sent you." Chief Ronn just stares at Hector while being hit by a lighting attack. Hector yells again, "WHO SENT YOU, TRIBESMAN?" and again hits him with lighting.

"Enough, Hector, you have more important things to attend to. I will get what we need from this one. Now, ready the next step in our plan."

"Yes, Master, I'll go ready the Magi for the next Great War, hahahaha."

"Brother and sisters of the Magi bloodline, what you been hearing is true; yes, the beacon on the hilltop of the Tribesmen has been lit, and yes, they prepare themselves for war, so we must be ready ourselves. Ready the army of the Magi. Enchanters, we will need you to make enchanted weapons for those in our kingdom who wish to fight who have no magic and also for the common folk who wish to fight as well. We leave in five days, and Wizards, Mages, Witches and Warlocks, go home be with your family, and remember: We are at WAR.

The Unseen Hand

"Master, did you get what we needed from him? Because he looks dead."

"Ohh no, Hector, he is not dead, and yes, I got what I needed. Did you do what you needed it to do?"

"Yes, Master, I have done all you asked; all the Magis are readying for war, and we march in five days. I have already sent a group of our risen Magis to attack the Tribesmen to provoke them, and I sent the army to attack the Zion and the Tribesmen. When the Tribesmen get here, the Zions will be battling with the remaining tribes-people that are left at their village, then we will attack with our risen army to wipe out the Zion and those Tribesmen and then we will head to the mountain and make all magic bloodline surrender and choose to follow the Necromancer or die.

"Good boy, Hector; now leave. I have many things to get done here. You have strong will, Tribesman. I couldn't break you, but with magic, I can read your mind, and for my old friend Mana, I can't wait till we see one another again."

"Molath, are you there? Molath, come in; Molath contact me as soon as possible. If any one harms my advisor, I will bring the Army of Five Kingdoms down upon them." The holograph disappears.

Molath walks out from a dark corner with an evil look in his eye and with a smile.

The Village of the True Born...

"Hiku, scouts reported that we have a large group of Magis heading straight for the Smith Tribe, and the Zion is building a base in the west. What should we do?"

Hiku then says, "Rain and 50 others are going to head for the Smith Tribe. Send word to the other tribe to send whatever men they can to support the west border. Keno, you will lead 200 True Borns to the border. Do not let the west borders fall; protect it at all cost."

"I know, Hiku, and who died and made you chief anyways? Also, for the record, I'm doing this for the True Born, not 'cause you told me to."

Hiku says, "Keno," and then both of them nod their head and head out. "We are heading for the eastern mountain to join up with the rest of our brothers and sisters. Let's move out," yells Hiku.

Back on Secret Hill...

Gordon returns to the Secret Hill to find that they weren't only attacked by Magi, but by their own people who had been dead during the past hundred years. Then Gordon is attacked by his lover, and he strikes her down before he even notices who it is. After the fog settles, Gordon sees that he has struck his wife, who had passed away a year ago from sickness. Gordon eyes fill with rage and his mind becomes lost because of what he saw and had done then he said with anger.

"WHEN DID THIS HAPPEN? HOW COULD THIS HAPPEN?" As his voice declined, he continues to say, "They were all dead… Why are they all here? What is going on? Damn magic, it has to be magic. I'm going to kill all those magic users if it's the last thing I do, you'll see; I'll show you what you get when you mess with me and my feelings. You'll see, you all will see—raahhhhhh!"

Rain

"All right, men, who's ready to smash some Magis' skulls?"

The 50 True Born shout, "SMASH 'UM."

"Let's ready our blades, and ready yourself for war!"

"We are True Born," the men all roar. "YEAH!"

A horn blows in the distance but near, then seconds after that, a large group walked out from the tree line and marched towards the Smith Tribe. Fireballs and arrows fall from the sky, then Rain yells, "Smith Tribe, shields up! Now ready your arrows and fire, next row fire, final row fire! True Born, let's show them what we made of!"

Fifty true born rush towards their enemy, facing a thousand men; they rush with pride and joy in their eyes and on their faces. When their metal clashes against their enemies' weapons, the warriors fight with everything that was taught to them. The bodies of their enemy fall 20-plus to one, and as the clashing continues, another horn blows from nearby, and a group from the Chiefess' tribe appears behind the enemy with 100 of their tribe warriors on horses.

"Charge forward and assist Rain!" they yell.

After Rain and the warriors on horseback eradicate the enemy and secure the safety of the Smith Tribe, one of the warriors on horseback tells Rain, "I'm glad we made it on time, but for us, we must ride on to aid the west fortress."

"Good luck, True Born," then the 100 horsemen ride towards the west.

Keno

Keno arrives at the western fortress that guards the border from the west entering the north.

"All right, True Born, ready defenses, load the barrels with javelins, and what tribe is here on watch?"

"I'm in charge here, I'm the second son of Chief Razor, Nathaniel."

"Nathaniel, how many men do you have here with you?" Keno asks.

Nathaniel responds, "There are 500 of us, but we don't take orders from you, True Born, and why are you early? It's not your watch, so tell me why me and my men shouldn't be hostile towards you."

"Enough of your ego, Nathaniel. We are all at war, not with one another, but against the Magi and possibly with Zion. I was sent here by the first son of Chief Ronn, Hiku, 'cause our scouts reported that Zion was making a base of some sort on land, and if it's war they want, then we need to hold this position till we fall or they fall, and please tell me that we have something to deal with them damn flyers."

Nathaniel smiles then says, "You control your men, and I'll control mine, okay? And also, we will be handling the new weapon we got from the Smith Tribe. Leave it to us to handle the flyers and more.

"Well, we True Borns do love the front line. Just be ready when it's time, Nathaniel."

Old Alpha

"Alphas 3, 4, 5, on me."

"Roger Alpha Leader."

Alpha Leader looks at that transport ship. It's big enough to move a whole army.

"Alpha Leader, look it's 2."

"Now is not a good time to deal with him. 3 and 4, make your way to the armory, get us some wings, and meet us at the south point of Zion. Me and 5 will go to the throne room and inform our leader of our finding. Alphas ready?"

"READY!"

"Move out."

"Alright, just up ahead should be the armory."

"Halt why ain't the both of you on board with the first wave?"

Alpha 3 responds, "We are on guard patrol."

"Guard patrol, huh? Then why do you have clothes of an officer? And by the looks of it, a high officer. Hands in the air or else I'll be forced to fry you both. Now, I'll ask you again: why are you here and not in there? Are you deserting?"

Alpha 4 replies, "Fine, we were just getting in a last few runs, if you know what I mean, before going off to war. I can show you our stash and where we keep the good stuff; you can have it all to yourself once we board."

"Now you're talking," responded to the guard. "Let's hurry; show me the stash."

"It's in the armory, let's be on our way."

"Okay, where is it?"

"It's right here." Then *boom!* Alpha 4 punches the guard's lights out and grabs what they went there for, but what they see blows their mind. "We must inform Alpha Leader ASAP." Then both of them headed south of Zion.

Meanwhile, Alpha Leader and 5 have managed to slip past the guards unnoticed and have made it to the throne room, where Alpha Leader and the King of Zion are discussing the matter at hand.

"My King, as you can see, we have been fooled by an enemy that we don't know of, and by the look on your face, it seems that you already have an idea of who it is, so what is the King's orders?"

The King says, "Tell the people of Zion who went below to hold their ground at the fortress and to not advance upon the Tribesmen till further orders are given. We will hold our new foothold on land."

"But Your Majesty, did you see the ships that have been built?"

The King looks towards his right-hand man, and his right-hand man tells the King, "Three-fourths of Zion army is already on the ground and not only that, all communication to our ground forces has been cut off."

"Who gave that order?" the King yells with anger.

The right-hand man of the King tells him, "You gave the new Alpha Leader more power than you should have, and now he has an army and resources to be his own King."

The King sits down on his throne and asks, "How many of our men are here?"

"Only the Royal Guards, Your Highness.

"Ready a ship and the rest of our troops. We are going below, but I need you to stay and maintain Zion. Wait for my signal, then bring Zion down and the King's battalion."

"Yes, Your Highness," replies his advisor.

CHAPTER 5

The Start of the War Begins in the West

At the New Alpha Nation…

Alpha Leader holds a gathering with the army of Zion. In the fortress they had built for them, "Zion," he calls out, "we've been sitting in the sky for a hundred years, and we've been training to be the best just as long, and now our enemy has presented themselves, and they choose us to be their foe, but we will show them what Zion is capable of. 'Cause today, we create a new nation; today, we will shed the blood of our enemy. Today, we are not Zion, 'cause today, we all stand side by side in this battle and shed blood of our enemy next to one another. From this day forward, there are not only five Alphas 'cause from what I see we are, ALL ALPHAS! Will you march with me and show the word the New Alpha Nation, where everyone is an Alpha?"

The army of Zion roared in excitement chanting, "ALPHA, NATION, ALPHA, NATION."

"We march to the western border."

"King Alpha," one of the scouts shouts, "we have enemies near the back end of our fortress."

King Alpha replies, "Send 20,000 men to meet our enemy, and you will lead and command them, Commander Scotty."

"Yes, Your Majesty."

"Crush them then regroup with the rest of us. Let's give them a taste of our strength!"

Commander Scotty and his men set up on the west side of their base.

"Alright, front line, shield wall and laser spears forward; second and third line, ready your volley shots and fire on my command."

As they wait, they can hear loud growling noise and snarling sounds; everything goes silent. Then a loud roar comes from the direction of the growling and snarling noise, then the army of the undead rush forward towards Commander Scotty. Commander Scotty yells in hesitation, "Fire every one, fire and stop them!"

The front line fires their weapon they are holding till the enemy smashes against their shields, and they push and slash and fire their weapon at their enemy. Commander Scotty is frozen when he sees the enemy army crash against the front line and his men fall dead to the ground. He runs, yelling, "Retreat!" Some broke formation retreating back to the fortress, while others died battling the enemy while trying to retreat, then a brave soldier yells out to the front line, "We will hold the enemies, my front line Alphas, so our brothers can escape! Front line, push!"

Then the whole front line with their shields up close and locked with each other roar and begin there advance moving forward.

"This is the second ranger line. We will also stay and provide the front line with support. All rangers, shoot to kill, and you, soldier, inform King Alpha there is a whole army coming from this direction. Let's just hope he's not engaged with the border line."

The West Border

Keno looks towards the west and sees a flock of birds scattering while flying in the sky from a distance then yells out to the tribesmen, "Our enemy is close! Ready the defense, True Borns, take out anyone who is not Tribe Born!"

The tribesmen ready themselves for battle, loading and adjusting their range weapon, setting up a weapon station and ballistics, then the 200 True Born warriors push and shove one another for a spot on the front line, and the hundred calvary riders wait in the back for their signal to attack, 1,500 warriors ready to operate the defenses weapon and defend it, all of them ready, all of them calm in their own way, all of them excited even while they look at 30,000 men who stand in front of them.

King Alpha raises his hand, and as soon as his hand goes down, his army rushes forward. A loud shout comes from the border line, "FIRE!" The Tribesmen do not hesitate to answer back when their enemy advances, the the catapult releases, making a loud singing noise before launching the rock into the air towards the oncoming enemy, then the sound of a silent but fast-paced weapon is also being fired at the enemy.

The Alpha Nation Army charges in and ignores their disadvantage and attempts to breach the walls, but when they reach the wall, True Born warriors stand waiting in the front of the walls with excitement and rush their enemy as soon as they get close. The sound of metal clashing metal fills the air, and so does the scent of blood. Some of the enemy army gets past the True Born warriors when their number falls from 200 to 70 after the first two hours of the battle. The enemy enters the town, but without the enemy knowing, a fire arrow is shot into the sky to signal the cavalry.

The cavalry rushes through the town like a wave and takes out anyone who passes the last of the True Borns who continue to stand their ground and refuse to give up. The battle goes on for hours, then finally King Alpha calls the retreat. After hearing the report about Commander Scotty and what took place, King Alpha sets up camp in front of the west borders and out of range of his enemies' weapons. He sits down and exhales, then says to himself, "Checkmate."

Keno stands and watches as his enemy sets up camp, then walks back into town and gathers the tribesmen who are left after the battle. Keno tells his fellow tribes-people about their enemy, about them setting up camp and how they might attack again at any moment.

"We must be on our guard, and we will hold the border, nothing more. We don't need to lose anymore warriors on secret mission to try and kill their King. We hold the border and send an owl to the tribe leaders to inform them about this."

The Brave Alpha

Hours after the retreat from the battle with the army of the undead, the front line and the secondary rangers managed to get back to their fortress with minimum losses and the undead army right on their tail. Inside of their fortress there is a narrow path with walls 10 feet high along its path way and extended 10 yards down. The secondary ranger squad positions themselves on the front walls and the walls along the pathway taking the high ground, and after the front line closes the gate to the fortress, they make their way to the end of the path and make a shield wall, getting ready for their enemy.

As they wait, the gates to the fortress shakes and the sound of their enemies' weapons smashing against it echo, and then comes the noise of the wood breaking and splitting, the sound of their snarling and growling, and the shouting from above them. The rangers yell, "Keep firing ranges; don't let up!"

Then finally, the loud crashing sound of the gate being tore down is heard. For a few seconds in that moment, everything goes quiet and moves in slow motion, then the sound of their heartbeats thump louder than normal. Finally, a soldier in the middle of the shield wall yells out, "SHIELDS AT THE READY!"

The whole front line calls out, "READY!" then shouts "Aaaah!"

Again, the sound of metal clashing against metal repeats itself like before; shields being smashed and bashed upon by their enemy weapons, the front line roars and slashes, pushes, and keeps piling up their enemies' bodies, but as time keeps passing by and being fatigued from the battle before, one at a time, their shields fall to the ground, filled with blood and dents. Then a loud shout comes from the top of the wall…

"Rangers, draw your weapons!" then the sound of all the rangers' daggers being unsheathed fills the air. All the rangers yelled out, "For ALPHA NATION!" before jumping off the wall and into battle. When the front line sees what the rangers have done, they charge forward but are stopped by a line of rangers, who tell them to, "Get to our Alpha King! He needs his shield wall, go, front line, for the Alpha nation!"

The front line stands straight up and replies, "For Alpha Nation!" then say, "See you soon, brothers."

Then the rangers ran towards the battle. The front line turns around and heads for the west border.

The King of Zion

Delta leader yells out, "Look down below, there are bodies all over the ground!" and as King Treon looks down, he sees bodyie all over the ground and as the clouds clear up under Zion, King Treon sees what he was hoping was not true. Then he tells Alpha Team to, "Scan the battlefield to see if there're any of our people down there."

"Dead or alive, bring them back?"

"Yes," King Treon replies.

The Alpha Team departs and searches the battlefield and makes trips back and forth from Zion with their fallen comrades in their hand.

King Treon walks into his room and shuts his door then pulls out a stone from his crown and places it on the ground then grabs a torch and puts it on the stone. As soon as the flames touch the stone, a hologram pops up, and King Treon says, "Long time no see, old friend."

A man turns around and says, "I see you got the message I sent to you. Do you have any information on this, and is it true?"

King Treon sighs and says, "Molath is back, and it looks like he has mastered the forbidden art known as Necromancy."

The man in the hologram responds with, "What proof do you have, Treon?"

King Treon tells him, "As of right now, I'm landing Zion, and below me is risen…"

Alpha Leader bursts in and tells King Treon, "All the bodies on the battlefield are coming back to life. We gotta land Zion somewhere else, Your Highness."

King Treon turns to the hologram and says, "I'll see you soon, old friend," and then picks up the stone and places it back on his crown and walks back out of his room.

As King Treon steps out, he sees Delta, Bravo, Charlie, and Alpha Teams fighting with the dead Zion soldiers from the battlefield below. King Treon draws his sword, walks towards the fight, and cuts off the head from five undead soldiers then tells all the squad, "Cut their heads off! It's the only way to kill them, and we will continue to take this path till we see a clearing. Alpha Team, scout ahead and see what's waiting for us."

"Yes, Your Highness."

Back to the border…

One day has passed since King Alpha has halted his attack on the western border. He sits and continues to try and come up with a plan of action but sees no way out being trapped in the middle of an army and a well-fortified border defense. From the west, he sees the front line marching towards him in a hurry.

When the front line reaches King Alpha, they tell him that the army from the west has overrun the fortress and is on their way. The front line soldier who has been leading them while in battle tells his King the only way is to make a truce and combine forces with the tribes-people who defend the border.

King Alpha turns to tells him that they already had attacked the border, and he doesn't believe that there can be a truce between them now, "But I'm glad you made it back, front line. I will need you to hold the front one more time, head to the west and make whatever perpetration you need to defend it."

The front line heads to the west and prepares themselves for the upcoming battle that is to come, then moments later, they see something approaching from the sky. The front line readies themselves.

"Zion," one of the men yells, "look it's a Zion ship."

King Treon lands the Zion ship on the south side of their camp and walks towards his people, but then all the sudden, the Alpha army draws there weapons upon their old king.

King Treon stands there with a puzzled look on his face as he looks around and sees what surrounds him, then says, "Where is your Alpha Leader?"

A soldier who was amongst those who stood in front of King Treon yells out, "It's King Alpha to you," then all the sudden, Delta, Bravo, Charlie, and Alpha step in front of King Treon with their weapons at the ready and tell them, "Back off, traitors, or it will be your head that will leave your shoulders."

King Alpha walks up to King Treon and tells him, "Well, hello, old King. What brings you here?"

Alpha Leaders sees Alpha 2 and takes a step towards him and says in an angry tone of voice, "You're Alpha King? Why? Why would you betray Zion, ALPHA 2."

"It's Alpha King; remember that, you alphas of Zion. Besides we are Alpha Nation now, not Zion, and by the looks of things, you're outnumbered, King Treon."

"Are you blind? We are all outnumbered; we are all in danger, and by the looks of things, you are surrounded. Let's go, Zion, we go to the border. It's a good thing you used your own banner and not Zion's. Good luck Alpha Nation."

TO BE CONTINUED…

CPSIA information can be obtained
at www.ICGtesting.com
Printed in the USA
LVHW082333170422
716440LV00014BA/1123

9 781636 616049